The Gingerbread Man

Retold by Carol North
Illustrated by John Nez

A GOLDEN BOOK • NEW YORK

Western Publishing Company, Inc., Racine, Wisconsin 53404

Once upon a time there was a little old woman and a little old man. They lived happily in a little house by the woods.

One day the little old woman wanted to surprise her husband. Do you know what she did? She made him a Gingerbread Man!

After she had trimmed the dough, the little old woman popped the Gingerbread Man into the oven to bake.

But when she peeked into the oven later to
see if the Gingerbread Man was done, he
jumped up and ran out the door.

"Stop! Stop!" cried the little old woman.
"Stop! Stop!" cried the little old man.

The Gingerbread Man laughed and called out, "Run, run—as fast as you can. You can't catch me, I'm the Gingerbread Man!"

The Gingerbread Man ran on until he met a
bunny.
"Stop! Stop!" cried the bunny. "I want to
eat you."

The Gingerbread Man laughed and called
out, "Run, run—as fast as you can. You can't
catch me, I'm the Gingerbread Man! I've run
away from a little old woman and a little old
man, and I can run away from you, I can, I can."

The bunny ran after the Gingerbread Man, but he couldn't catch him.

The Gingerbread Man ran on until he met a
bear cub.

"Stop! Stop!" cried the bear cub. "I want to
eat you."

The Gingerbread Man laughed and called out, "Run, run—as fast as you can. You can't catch me, I'm the Gingerbread Man! I've run away from a little old woman and a little old man, a bunny, and I can run away from you, I can, I can."

The bear cub ran and ran after the Gingerbread Man, but he couldn't catch him.

Next the Gingerbread Man met a
woodcutter.
"Stop! Stop!" cried the woodcutter. "I want
to eat you."

The Gingerbread Man laughed and called out, "Run, run—as fast as you can. You can't catch me, I'm the Gingerbread Man! I've run away from a little old woman and a little old man, a bunny, and a bear cub, and I can run away from you, I can, I can."

The woodcutter ran after the Gingerbread Man, but he couldn't catch him.

No one could catch the Gingerbread Man. Not the little old woman or the little old man, not the bunny, and not the bear cub. Not even the woodcutter. The Gingerbread Man ran on and on.

But then the Gingerbread Man came to a river. He looked over his shoulder at everyone chasing him. "Oh, dear, what am I to do?" he said.

Just then a sly old fox came out of the
bushes. "Hello," said the fox, "I can help. Hop
on my tail, and I will carry you across."

The Gingerbread Man saw that he had no
time to lose, so he hopped onto the fox's tail,
and into the water they went.

When they were halfway across, the fox said, "The water is deep here. You had better get on my back."

So the Gingerbread Man got onto the fox's back.

Soon the fox said, "The water is getting even deeper. Jump on my head."
So the Gingerbread Man jumped onto the fox's head.

When they were almost across, the fox said, "The water is deepest here. You had better jump on my nose."

And the Gingerbread Man did. Then the fox opened his mouth wide and...smack, smack, yum, yum! That was the end of the Gingerbread Man.

But then, gingerbread men are made to be eaten.